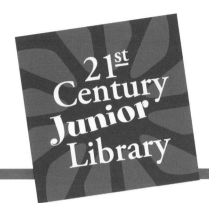

21st
Century
Junior
Library

FAIRNESS

by Lucia Raatma

CHERRY LAKE PUBLISHING * ANN ARBOR, MICHIGAN

8-09
23-

CHERRY LAKE
Publishing

Published in the United States of America by Cherry Lake Publishing
Ann Arbor, Michigan
www.cherrylakepublishing.com

Reading Adviser: Cecilia Minden-Cupp, PhD, Literacy Consultant

Photo Credits: Cover and page 4, ©Jupiterimages/Comstock Images; cover and page 6,
©iStockphoto.com/bonniej; page 8, ©Norma Cornes, used under license from Shutterstock,
Inc.; cover and page 10, ©Jupiterimages/Creatas Images; cover and page 12, ©JustASC,
used under license from Shutterstock, Inc.; page 14, ©Kirill Kurashov, used under license from
Shutterstock, Inc.; page 16, ©Corbis Premium RF/Alamy; page 18, ©Bubbles Photolibrary/
Alamy; page 20, ©JUPITERIMAGES/PIXLAND/Alamy

LIBRARY OF CONGRESS CATALOGING-IN-PUBLICATION DATA
Raatma, Lucia.
Fairness / by Lucia Raatma.
    p. cm.—(Character education)
Includes index.
ISBN-13: 978-1-60279-322-4
ISBN-10: 1-60279-322-0
1. Fairness—Juvenile literature. I. Title. II. Series.
BJ1533.F2R33 2009
179'.9—dc22   2008030910

*Cherry Lake Publishing would like to acknowledge the work of
The Partnership for 21st Century Skills.
Please visit www.21stcenturyskills.org for more information.*

CONTENTS

The playground is just one place where you may need to take turns.

What Is Fairness?

"Hey, it's my turn," Joe said as Brian cut in front of him. "I was next!"

Brian started to argue but then stopped. "You're right. You were here before me. You've been waiting in line," he answered.

"Thanks for being fair," Joe replied. "When we're done with the slide, let's try the swings!"

Playing fair means treating the other team the way you like to be treated.

When you are fair, you follow the rules. You don't play **favorites** with your friends or family. You treat others the way you would like to be treated. You also think about how your actions will **affect** other people.

Look!

Watch a group of friends play a game that you don't know how to play. Try to figure out what the rules of the game are. Were you able to figure out the rules just by watching others play?

Have you ever spilled something? Did you admit your mistake or did you try to blame someone else?

Being Fair with Others

You can be fair to the people around you in lots of ways. One way is to not blame others for a **mistake** you make. At home, you might forget to complete a chore. **Admit** that you made a mistake and finish your chore.

Create!

Write a story about someone who has been treated unfairly. Think about what you've seen in school or on the playground. Is it ever fair to treat one group of people differently from others?

Raising hands in class helps make sure everyone gets a turn to speak.

Another way to be fair is to always follow the rules. At school, the rule may be to line up for lunch or the bathroom. Don't try to cut ahead of others. Don't run to be first in line.

When you run ahead or cut in line you aren't being fair to others. You are also breaking your school's rule about lining up.

A baseball field has lines on it. They help players follow the rules about whether a ball is fair or foul.

Take turns when you play games with your friends. And remember, a fair person does not **cheat**. If you say that a ball was "out" when it really was "in," that's cheating. Others may not want to play with you if you don't play fairly.

Ask Questions!

If you are unsure about the rules of a game, ask someone before you begin. Discuss the rules with the other players. Make sure that everyone understands and agrees. Then everyone will have a fair chance to play the game.

How would you feel if someone blamed you for something you didn't do?

A fair person tells the truth. Telling a lie to cover up a mistake is not honest. It is a form of cheating. And someone else may be blamed for your mistake.

A fair person is honest with others. Maybe your sister didn't understand the rules of a game you were playing. You were able to beat her using the rules. Is that fair?

Sharing chores at home is one way to be fair.

Helping Others to Be Fair

Being fair is important. You can help others to be fair by setting a good example. Maybe you and your brother can share chores. Work together to find ways to share the chores fairly. Use a chart to help remind you both whose turn it is to do a chore.

Have you ever seen someone being bullied on the playground? What do you think you could have done to help?

You might see someone being treated unfairly at school. Maybe it is a student who is new or doesn't have many friends. Maybe the other kids are teasing him for being different.

How can you help? Ask friends if they would like to be treated that way. Or ask a teacher or other adult to help. No one should be treated unfairly.

How can you practice fairness today?

When you are fair, your **relationships** with other people are better. Your friends like being around you. And your family knows they can trust you. If you act fairly with others, they will most likely be fair with you, too!

Think!

Remember a time when you were treated unfairly. How did it make you feel? Would you ever want to make someone else feel that way?

GLOSSARY

admit (ad-MIT) to agree that something is true; to confess to something

affect (uh-FEKT) to change someone or something

cheat (CHEET) to act dishonestly to win a game or get what you want

favorites (FAY-vuh-rits) people who receive special treatment

mistake (muh-STAKE) an error or misunderstanding

relationships (ri-LAY-shuhn-ships) the ways in which people get along with one another

FIND OUT MORE

BOOKS

Finn, Carrie. *Kids Talk About Fairness*. Minneapolis: Picture Window Books, 2007.

Rosenthal, Amy Krouse, and Tom Lichtenheld (illustrator). *It's Not Fair!* New York: HarperCollins Publishers, 2008.

WEB SITES

Goodcharacter.com—Fairness/Justice
www.goodcharacter.com/pp/fairness.html
For a list of ways to be a fair person and links to other character resources

PBS Kids—WayBack: It's Not Fair!
pbskids.org/wayback/fair/fighters/index.html
Learn about some people who stood up for what is right

INDEX

ABOUT THE AUTHOR

Lucia Raatma has written dozens of books for young readers. They are about famous people, historical events, ways to stay safe, and other topics. She lives in Florida's Tampa Bay area with her husband and their two children.